THE CAPTAIN'S HAT

$2.50

by Deb Mercier

Illustrated by Faythe Mills

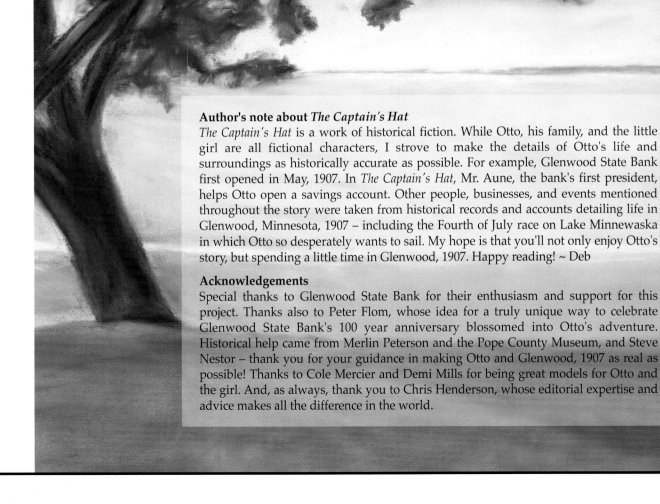

First Printing 2007

ISBN 978-0-9799410-0-9

Printed in Canada

The pictures in this book
were done in soft pastels.

MP
Minnewaska Press
Glenwood, Minnesota

Author's note about _The Captain's Hat_

The Captain's Hat is a work of historical fiction. While Otto, his family, and the little girl are all fictional characters, I strove to make the details of Otto's life and surroundings as historically accurate as possible. For example, Glenwood State Bank first opened in May, 1907. In _The Captain's Hat_, Mr. Aune, the bank's first president, helps Otto open a savings account. Other people, businesses, and events mentioned throughout the story were taken from historical records and accounts detailing life in Glenwood, Minnesota, 1907 – including the Fourth of July race on Lake Minnewaska in which Otto so desperately wants to sail. My hope is that you'll not only enjoy Otto's story, but spending a little time in Glenwood, 1907. Happy reading! ~ Deb

Acknowledgements

Special thanks to Glenwood State Bank for their enthusiasm and support for this project. Thanks also to Peter Flom, whose idea for a truly unique way to celebrate Glenwood State Bank's 100 year anniversary blossomed into Otto's adventure. Historical help came from Merlin Peterson and the Pope County Museum, and Steve Nestor – thank you for your guidance in making Otto and Glenwood, 1907 as real as possible! Thanks to Cole Mercier and Demi Mills for being great models for Otto and the girl. And, as always, thank you to Chris Henderson, whose editorial expertise and advice makes all the difference in the world.

In remembrance of Peter Flom, who leaves behind a legacy
of kindness, humor, and generosity of spirit.

For Dad - *DM*
For Egan, Demi, Alayna, Grayson, and Canon - *FM*

$\mathcal{T}$he summer of 1907 was just a breath away, or so it seemed to Otto Arneson. As soon as the dismissal bell rang, he burst through the doors of the schoolhouse, leaped down the steps, and raced through the village as fast as his eight-year-old legs could carry him. He rounded the corner onto Minnesota Avenue, and there was the lake, a vast and sparkling sapphire spread beneath the equally blue sky. Otto streaked past Callighan's Hardware and didn't even pause to peek in the windows of Simmon's Pool Hall.

Mr. Reeves, just coming out of his office above McKinley Mercantile called out, "Where's the fire, young Arneson?" But Otto was already gone. Smith's Café and White's Grocery passed in a blur of brick and mortar.

The fresh, cool air of an early May afternoon pushed at his back. Soon, Otto could hear the rhythmic rush of waves breaking on the shore. They hit once every eight steps. *Whoosh*-two-three-four-five-six-seven-eight, *whoosh*-two-three-four-five-six-seven-eight, Otto's feet flew. Panting, he skidded to a stop at the pavilion, grabbing on to one of the wooden posts to avoid tumbling down the bank and into the still frigid water of Lake Minnewaska.

"Pa!" he called, waving. "Pa! Up here!"

A man stopped working on a sailboat, looked up, and waved. Otto slid down the bank.

His father squinted at him in the bright sunshine. "How on earth did you get here so fast, Otto?" His face darkened. "You didn't leave school early, did you?"

"No, sir!" said Otto. "I waited until Miss McLachlan rang the bell. I just ran is all, honest."

Otto's father nodded. School was serious business. Being a railroad switchman was fine for him, he always said, but he wanted better for his sons.

"*W*ell? Is she ready?" asked Otto, almost dancing in anticipation.

"Nearly," said Otto's father. He patted the sailboat's hull. "Your brother and I will take the *Jolly Kate* on her first voyage of the season as soon as he arrives."

Otto's heart sank. He looked at his shoes.

Otto's father sighed. "Otto –"

"I just thought," said Otto, "that maybe this time I could sail with you. I did get here first," he added hopefully. "And with the race coming up on the Fourth of July, you'll need all the help you can get, right?"

"Otto, we've talked about this before. You're not big enough to go sailing just yet. Especially in a race. Give it another year or two. Perhaps then."

Other kids began trickling into the pavilion, as they often did after school. Otto's brother, William, made his way down the bank in a couple of graceful, sliding steps. Will made everything look easy.

"Hi Pa, hi Squirt," he said. Squirt was Will's nickname for Otto. And unfortunately, being six years older and a foot and a half taller, he could get away with it. "Is she ready?"

"Ready as she'll ever be," said Otto's father. "Question is, are you ready?"

"Yes, sir!" said Will.

Otto's father laughed. "That's 'yes, Captain' today."

Otto sat on the bank and watched until the *Jolly Kate's* sail was just a white dot on the horizon, frustration boiling in his stomach like a hot, clenched fist. He was big enough. He *could* sail the *Jolly Kate*. He knew he could. If only he could convince his father...

Normally, Otto would have hitched a ride on one of the horse-drawn taxis running up to Soo Hill where he and his family lived. But today, Otto walked slowly back through town.

He stopped in front of Johnson's Drug Store, horrified by the advertisement for Castoria plastered in the window. That was the stuff his mother made him swallow every time he felt ill. After just a few doses, Otto was much more careful not to mention those things anymore.

Across the street, the Fremad building was doing its best to live up to its reputation as the busiest corner in town. Things were a bit slow on Thursday afternoon, but come Saturday night, the corner would be hopping – full of shoppers, opera house and bank patrons, men disappearing into the mysterious Masonic Hall upstairs, and farmers come to barter their wares.

A girl, maybe five or six years old, sat outside the Fremad building, thin arms wrapped around her drawn-up knees. Even from where he stood, Otto could see grubby little toes sticking out from underneath her long, patched skirt. A taxi broke Otto's view with a clatter of hooves. When it had passed, the girl was walking away, holding the hand of a tired-looking woman. The little girl looked back over her shoulder at Otto and offered him a shy smile.

*O*tto scowled and turned away. He scuffed his feet as he walked up the street, hands shoved in his pockets. *There must be something*, he thought, *something that will convince Pa I'm big enough to sail.*

And, like a gift from heaven, there it was. A captain's hat, sharp as you please, perched in the window of Thacker & Bros. department store. It was a deep, navy blue with a gold, embroidered anchor on the front, and a short, no-nonsense bill. It was a hat worthy of Captain Ahab himself. Suddenly, a plan began to unfold in Otto's mind. He pressed his nose to the glass and shaded his eyes to see if Mr. Thacker had posted the price. He had. Otto gulped and backed up, nearly running into Dr. Shipstead, the dentist, out from his office up the street for some air.

"I say, boy, what's the trouble?" he asked. " You look like you've seen a ghost."

"No sir, excuse me, sir," said Otto, swallowing again. "Just a price."

"Ah," said the dentist. "That'll do it, too." He whistled as he continued down the street.

The price tag on the captain's hat – the hat Otto was sure would convince his father he was big enough to sail – read two dollars and fifty cents. That was more than his mother had paid for her new rocking chair!

Otto started home again, passing the newly opened Glenwood State Bank. The two-story building towered above its one-story neighbors. Everything from the fancy etched glass at the top of the window to the grand stone archway reminded Otto of money. *How in the world am I going to come up with $2.50?* he thought. Absently, he kicked a bottle someone had left on the sidewalk. It made a hollow *clink* as it rapped up against the bank's front step. He stared at the bottle, and a smile spread across his face. In one movement, he scooped the bottle from the ground and took off at a run.

Twenty minutes later, he stood in front of the bank again, back from the pop and wine factory and just a little out of breath. Instead of a bottle, he held one, beautiful, shiny penny. He peered into the shadowed archway at the bank's enormous wood carved door. The bank was closed for the day. But tomorrow, Otto decided, he and the bank had business to attend to.

Otto squirmed in his seat at school so much the next day that Miss McLachlan finally threw her hands up in exasperation. "Mr. Arneson," she said. "Do you have somewhere you'd rather be?" Otto jumped. "No, ma'am," he said, and tried not to think about the penny resting in his pocket.

Finally, finally, Miss McLachlan excused the children, and once again, Otto flew through the town. Important looking men with their suits and mustaches strode into the bank's stone archway and disappeared behind the wooden door. Otto gulped and patted his pocket to make sure his penny was still there.

"Hello," said a small voice to his left. The girl in the patched skirt was sitting against the bank's stony front, knees drawn up. She squinted up at Otto.

"Hello," said Otto, distracted. He was trying to work up the courage to go into the bank.

"I like this building, don't you?" asked the girl.

Now Otto was starting to get annoyed. "I suppose," he said.

"It's tall and strong. Like Papa used to be," said the girl. "But he died."

"Oh. I'm sorry," said Otto. He felt a twinge of sympathy. His own uncle had died just last year. Otto shuffled his feet, feeling awkward. The girl was still staring at him.

Just to say something he asked, "What are you doing here? Where's your mother?"

"Over there, I think," said the girl, waving her hand across the street. "She's looking for work. Maybe some supper. She's not feeling well, you know. I'd very much like to go to school. Do you go to school?"

"Yes," said Otto.

"Oh! What's it like? Do you get to draw and write do 'rithmetic? Can you read?" rattled off the little girl, her eyes shining.

Otto's sympathy scattered in the face of all her words. "Yes – and some – I have to go," he said. He shook his head and marched into the shadow of the stone arch. He pulled at the handle of the wooden door. It didn't budge. His cheeks burned, and he put all of his might into opening the heavy door.

The little girl popped her head around the arch's entrance, watching Otto. "Do you need help?" she asked.

"No!" snapped Otto.

The little girl sighed. "That's what Mama always says." She skipped over to the door, light as a feather on her bare feet, and added her spindly arms to Otto's efforts. The door opened just enough, and Otto slipped inside, the girl's "Goodbye" cut off as the door quickly closed behind him.

$\mathcal{T}$he bank smelled of dry paper, cool brick, and freshly oiled wood. He cleared his throat and walked nervously toward the cashier's window. A younger man with close-cropped blond hair stared down at Otto. "Yes?" he said.

"I'd –," Otto squeaked. He cleared his throat again. "I'd like to open an account, please."

The young banker raised his eyebrows.

"I've already got a penny, you see," said Otto, placing his penny on the counter. He looked up hopefully. "I need to save $2.49 more, and my Pa says we should always give new businesses in town a fair shake which is why I came here instead of the old banks and your building is really grand." Otto's cheeks burned once again.

"I see," said the cashier. "How old are you?"

"Nearly nine," said Otto.

"I see." said the cashier again. "You do realize that you need your father's permission to open an account?"

Otto's face fell. "Oh, but that would ruin everything!" he said. "My father can't know about the account because it's a surprise!" Others in the bank looked Otto's way at his pleading tone.

The cashier shook his head. "Keep your voice down, boy."

An older man with a thick, black mustache appeared behind the young banker, putting his hand on the cashier's shoulder. "Can I be of some assistance?" he asked.

"This boy says he wants to open an account, but doesn't have his father's permission. It's out of the question, sir."

"I'll be the judge of that, Mr. Kalton," said the man. His sharp, kind eyes appraised Otto. "And why, may I inquire, do you need to open an account, young man?"

Otto recognized him immediately. Everyone in town knew Mr. Aune, the new bank's president. Otto explained about the captain's hat, the *Jolly Kate* and the Fourth of July race. "I know I can earn enough by then, sir," said Otto, fairly dancing from foot to foot with earnestness. "And my Pa always says the safest place for your money is at the bank."

"Let me confer with my associate," said Mr. Aune. He spoke in hushed tones to another man with swept back, silver hair and an impressive salt-and pepper mustache, gesturing over to Otto. Otto tried his best to keep still.

Mr. Aune came back, his eyes twinkling. "Mr. Kalton. Mr. McCauley and I feel young Arneson's patronage will make a fine addition to the bank." He nodded to Otto. "Welcome to Glenwood State Bank."

Otto emerged from the bank some time later, blinking in the bright sunshine at the ledger in his hand. One cent. Only $2.49 to go. Shoving the ledger in his pocket, Otto set out to earn the captain's hat.

$\mathcal{B}$y the end of May, school had let out for the summer. Over the next month, Otto worked tirelessly, spending every spare minute scrounging up odd jobs around town. His first idea had been picking up more glass bottles – at a penny apiece, he couldn't go wrong. Unfortunately, the prime bottle spots were already staked out by boys older and bigger than Otto. Instead of combing the vacant lots where Andrew's Photography and the cigar factory used to be, he had to settle for weaving through the alleys. Once, he ran into the little girl from the front of the bank – she was looking for bottles, too.

"Hello, it's you again," she said, clutching a dirty bottle to her chest. "I found a bottle."

"I see that," said Otto, his eyes sweeping the alley ahead.

"I get a whole penny for it," she said.

"I know," said Otto, impatient to move on.

"Why are you looking for bottles?" asked the girl.

"What do you mean?"

"You already have shoes," said the girl, puzzled.

"Of course I have shoes," said Otto. He looked down at the girl's bare feet and felt his cheeks blaze.

"Mama says I need shoes to go to school."

"Oh."

"Well, see you," said the girl. She skipped down the alley like a scattering of leaves.

Otto looked at the bottles in his hands with a strange feeling in the pit of his stomach. *Must be nearly lunchtime*, he thought.

Down by the pavilion, his father and Will were just putting the *Jolly Kate* in the water for another run. Otto munched on his homemade lunch and watched with envy. He yearned to tell his father about his brilliant plan and ask him, "Am I big enough yet?" But he felt the plan should be secret – as if speaking it out loud would somehow make it all fall apart.

Every day, between odd jobs, Otto went back to Thacker's and looked in the front window, breathing a sigh of relief when the captain's hat was still there. He already felt as if it were his. And every day, right before closing time, Otto deposited his earnings for the day in his bank account, usually earning him a wink and a smile from Mr. Aune, as well. Sometimes it was only a few pennies; on a record day, Otto deposited nearly 20 cents.

When he'd exhausted the bottle option, Otto hit the livery stables. Between Mr. Hafstad, Mr. McLachlan, Mr. Helbing, and Mr. Beusing, Otto cleaned out enough stables to know that he never wanted to see another horse as long as he lived.

Otto carried bags at the hotels for small tips from travelers, too. The salesmen that displayed their wares at the New Minton, he was convinced, carried lead bricks in their cases.

Mrs. Miller wouldn't let Otto into her saloon, but Mr. Landing was willing to let Otto wash dishes at his restaurant for a day or two. Those days, Otto handed his money over at the bank with red and wrinkled hands, sore from hours of scrubbing.

$\mathcal{O}$ne day, while leaving the drug store after a particularly tough shift dragging boxes of the dreaded Castoria inside for Mr. Johnson, Otto nearly tripped over the little girl. She was sitting outside Johnson's in the same, ragged skirt, knees drawn up as usual. Not that Otto knew her well, but she seemed subdued, almost gloomy.

"Hello," said Otto, in what he hoped was a friendly voice.

The little girl looked up. "Oh, it's you," she said.

For lack of anything else to say, Otto asked, "Where's your mother today?"

"Home. She's not feeling well at all."

"Don't you have any uncles or aunts or anything?"

"No." The little girl shrugged. "Mama says Papa's my guardian angel now. But I don't know. Do you believe in angels?"

"Yes," said Otto, although he'd never seen one himself. On impulse he said, "Would you like to see my hat?"

The little girl shrugged again.

She stood up and followed Otto up the street. At Thacker's, Otto pointed to the captain's hat in the window. "When I buy that hat," he said, "my father's going to know I'm big enough to sail with him in the Fourth of July race."

"Oh!" cried the little girl, her face pressed to the window next to Otto's. "It's beautiful!"

Otto scowled. Beautiful wasn't exactly how he'd choose to describe it. Leave it to a girl to ruin a perfectly good hat.

"And this hat means you get to sail?" asked the little girl.

"Of course," said Otto. "You can't very well wear a captain's hat and not be a captain, can you?"

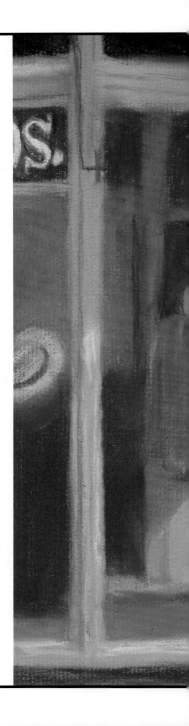

"I don't know," said the little girl. "I never met a captain." Her eyes got wide. "Do you smell that?" she asked. A customer stepped out of the next-door bakery. The smell of fresh baked bread followed him onto the sidewalk.

"It's just bread," said Otto.

"Yes, I know," said the little girl wistfully.

The little girl always seemed to make Otto's stomach feel weird. Suddenly, the hastily made sandwich he'd shoved in his pocket that morning didn't seem all that appetizing.

"Here," he said, offering the sandwich to the little girl.

"Oh I musn't!" she said. "You'll be hungry!" But her eyes never strayed from the sandwich.

"I ate a lot this morning," said Otto. "I'm not hungry. It'll just go to waste if you don't eat it."

"Mama does say we musn't waste," said the little girl. "Thank you."

"Well," said Otto, out of things to say. "Well, I hope your mother feels better."

The little girl nodded, already devouring the sandwich. Otto felt her eyes on him as he disappeared into the bank to make his daily deposit.

As July Fourth drew closer and closer, Otto got busier and busier. His bank account had grown to nearly the $2.50 he needed to finally buy the captain's hat. With his goal so close, Otto threw himself into work, staying home only long enough to eat, sleep, and take care of chores. At night, he dreamed of sailing. From time to time he saw the little girl around town. Her mother, he thought, really ought to tell her to take a bath. And she seemed to have the annoying habit of hitching up her skirt as if it didn't fit right. Otto didn't stop to talk, though. He was too busy carrying groceries, or cleaning out rental boats down by the pavilion.

Finally, finally, the day came when Otto went to make his final deposit.

"Hello, Mr. Kalton," he said, putting his coins on the counter.

"Deposit again today, Otto?" said Mr. Kalton, raising his eyebrows and smiling.

"Yes, sir," said Otto proudly. He took the battered ledger from his pocket. "And by my calculations, I should have..." he frowned at the ledger in concentration. "Two dollars and 51 cents."

Mr. Kalton checked Otto's figures. "I believe you're right."

Otto could scarcely believe he was saying the words. "I would like to withdraw two dollars and fifty cents, please." He could hardly stand still he was so excited. Mr. Kalton put the coins in a bag and handed it to Otto. Otto felt the weight of the money in his hands and grinned at Mr. Kalton.

*F*orgetting to be dignified, he called, "Thank you!" as he raced out the door. He plowed right into the little girl, who'd been waiting outside. She tumbled to the sidewalk with a squeak.

"I'm sorry," said Otto, helping her back to her feet. "Are you all right?" His hand almost closed around her stick-thin arm. Her hair was a mess, and her face was smudged with dirt.

"I'm all right," she said, hitching up her skirt. "I saw you go in. Are you going to be a captain now?"

"Yes," said Otto, surprised she'd remembered. Because he was in such a good mood, he asked, "Would you like to see me buy my hat?"

"Okay," said the little girl. She trailed behind Otto as he hurried down the walk to Thacker's. He took one last look at the captain's hat in the window, savoring the thought that he now had enough to buy it. He could almost feel the waves parting in front of the *Jolly Kate's* hull. He went to pull open the shop's door. Something made him pause and look back. The little girl wasn't following, like he'd expected. Instead, she was turned toward the bakery next door, her eyes closed, her chin trembling just the tiniest bit.

"What are you doing?" asked Otto.

The girl started. "Nothing," she said.

Otto shrugged and reached for the door again. Another something made him pause. "How's your mother?" he asked.

"She won't call on the doctor," said the little girl.

"What do you mean?" asked Otto.

"She won't call on the doctor. She says you don't take what you can't pay for." Again her chin trembled just the tiniest bit. "She promised she'd get better anyway."

"Oh," said Otto. He reached one more time for the door. He glanced at the captain's hat, still waiting for him just inside. He felt the weight of the money bag in his hand again, but it was a different kind of weight than the one he'd felt standing in the bank.

*S*lowly, he turned away from the store, and before he could change his mind, thrust the bag into the little girl's hands. Her eyes went wide.

"What are you doing?" she said.

"Just take it," said Otto. "Call on the doctor."

"But I musn't!" she said, looking distressed. "Mama said never, never, never take money for anything other than honest work."

Otto thought quickly. "Well," he said. "You did do honest work. You helped me open the door when I made my first penny. Without you, I might never have gotten in the bank in the first place."

The little girl's face broke into a huge smile. "I did help, didn't I?" she said. She looked at the bag of coins in her hand with disbelief. "Thank you."

Otto nodded, unable to say a word. He looked at the captain's hat in the window as if to say goodbye.

The little girl turned to leave, then turned back, clutching the bag tightly in her small fist. "I mightn't never met a captain before," she said. "But I think... I think I might've met an angel." She flashed a shy smile and took off at a run, her wild, tangled hair flying behind her.

Otto sighed, casting one, last, long look at the captain's hat in Thacker's window. He wasn't sorry for what he'd done, he knew that. But with the Fourth of July only a couple of days away, he'd never prove to his father now that he was big enough to sail.

Suddenly, a shadow fell across him. In the reflection of the window, Otto saw his father standing behind him. He turned around slowly, unsure of what to say.

"Nice hat," said his father.

"Yes, sir," said Otto.

"I saw what you did, Otto. And I know how hard you've been working to save up for that hat."

Otto's face grew pale. "But –"

Otto's father smiled. "People talk, son. Even young bankers." He inclined his head toward the captain's hat. "But I need to tell you something. It's not the hat that makes the man – it's the heart." He reached out and gave Otto's shoulder a squeeze. "I would be honored, Otto Arneson, if you would join my crew."

A gentle summer breeze tousled Otto's hair. "Yes, sir," he said. He grinned and looked toward the lake. For just a moment, he closed his eyes. He could already feel the cool spray on his face as the *Jolly Kate* sailed her way through the sun-kissed waves.